BATMAN

OCT - 2018

BATMAN™ SAYS THANK YOU

By May Nakamura
Illustrated by Patrick Spaziante
Batman created by Bob Kane with Bill Finger

Simon Spotlight
New York London Toronto Sydney New Delhi

SIMON SPOTLIGHT
An imprint of Simon & Schuster Children's Publishing Division
1230 Avenue of the Americas, New York, New York 10020
This Simon Spotlight paperback edition September 2018
All rights reserved, including the right of reproduction in whole or in part in any form.
SIMON SPOTLIGHT and colophon are registered trademarks of Simon & Schuster, Inc.
For information about special discounts for bulk purchases, please contact Simon & Schuster Special Sales at 1-866-506-1949 or business@simonandschuster.com.
Manufactured in the United States of America 0718 LAK
10 9 8 7 6 5 4 3 2 1
ISBN 978-1-5344-2543-9
ISBN 978-1-5344-2544-6 (eBook)

It is the end of another busy night in Gotham City. Batman and his super hero team have been working all through the night, and they are tired.

Batman sees the tired heroes and has an idea.

"I want to host a team dinner for us," Batman tells Robin. "Can you help me plan it?"

"Sure!" Robin says. "But why do you want to have a dinner?"
"It's a way to say thank you for everyone's hard work," Batman answers.

The next morning Robin is in charge of inviting the super heroes. "Hey, guys, come to the team dinner!" he shouts into his communication device.

Batman shakes his head. "Remember to speak politely when you're asking for something."

Robin tries again. "Please, we would be greatly humbled and honored, please, if you could join us for a team dinner, please."

"Something like that," Batman says.

Next, Batman and Robin decide the menu for the dinner.

"Can we make roast beef with gravy, and chicken pot pie, and French onion soup, and cheese soufflé?" Robin asks.

"You won't be able to fit into your suit afterward," Batman answers.

Alfred creates a grocery list. Then he straightens up Wayne Manor. He also retrieves the fancy teapots and silverware from a cabinet.

Batman asks Alfred if he needs help. Robin wonders why Batman is offering—Alfred is his butler!

"He may be my butler, but I want to help someone who always helps me," Batman says.

Alfred smiles. "Thank you, Master Wayne. Will you please carry these dishes to the dining room?"

Finally, it is time for the dinner. Nightwing arrives at the manor first. Then Green Arrow is right behind him.

The Flash is the last one to join the friends.
"If you're the Fastest Man Alive, why are you last?" Green Arrow jokes.

The super heroes sit down at the dinner table. Robin's mouth waters when he sees all the delicious food. He wants to dive in right away, but he knows he should wait until everyone has been served.

Batman stands. "Thank you all for coming to the dinner."
The other super heroes respond, "Thanks, Batman!"
Robin adds, "Let's eat!"

"So, Flash, what made you so late?" Green Arrow asks again. "Did you have to catch your breath or something? You're not much of a long-distance runner, are you?"

"Whatever Flash was doing, it was better than what you were up to," Nightwing jokes.

"Yeah, what makes you think I'll tell *you*?" the Flash adds.

Robin protests that teasing and jokes aren't polite at the dinner table. Being a team is about being kind to one another.

"We aren't being mean to each other," Nightwing says. "In fact, I owe it to Green Arrow for helping me look for Clayface at the history museum."

"That's nothing compared to the time you watched my back when we fought the Cyber Wolves," Green Arrow tells Nightwing. "Thanks, man."

"Nightwing even encouraged me when I had to run through the Penguin's force field," the Flash adds. "I really needed that."

The super heroes also thank Alfred. Alfred always keeps watch over the Batcave and Wayne Manor. He might not fight crime in the streets of Gotham City, but he is a member of the team, too.

Alfred announces, "Tonight's dessert is a caramel cheesecake. Would anyone care for some more tea?"

Just then the Bat-Signal appears in the sky. Batman jumps up. "Sorry, but dessert has to wait for another time. We need to go." Robin groans. "But I love cheesecake."

"Well, do any of you want to stay behind and miss the action?" Batman says.

Robin, Nightwing, Green Arrow, and the Flash look at one another. "Thank you, but no thank you!"

Once again it's up to Batman and his super hero team to save Gotham City. They wouldn't have it any other way.

PARTY PLANNING THE BATMAN WAY

Just like Batman, you can plan your own thank-you party for your friends and family. Follow these guidelines for a fun time.

BEFORE THE PARTY...

» Choose whom you want to invite. Don't forget to add Batman to your list!

» With an adult, decide where and when to host the event. Batman had the team dinner at home, but you can also go to a restaurant or park.

» Send invitations to your guests.

» Decide the menu with an adult. Make sure to ask your guests if they have any food allergies.

AT THE PARTY...

» Make sure the party space is nice and tidy.
  Add Batman-themed decorations!

» Offer to help with cooking or other preparations.

» Smile and greet all your guests.

» Don't start eating until everyone has their food.

» Remember your table manners. Chew with your
  mouth closed and try not to spill.

» Most important, say thank you!

WRITE A THANK-YOU NOTE

Thank-you notes are a great way to tell someone thank you. Here are four steps to help you write a thank-you note:

1. To begin your note, write "Dear" and then the name of the person you're thanking. This shows that you wrote the thank-you note just for them.

2. Say thank you. Don't forget to mention what you're thanking the person for— did the person do something nice? Did you receive a present? Write about why the person made you thankful!

3. When you're finished with the message, sign your name. Otherwise, the person won't know who sent the note!

4. Decorate your note with crayons, stickers, or stamps.

Great job! You've written a thank-you note!

THERE ARE MANY WAYS FOR YOU TO BE THANKFUL, JUST LIKE BATMAN:

 Count your blessings. Every day, think about the things you're thankful for.

 Give a gift to show how thankful you are. Even better, make a handmade card!

 Give back to your neighborhood. Help out at a soup kitchen or clean up litter on the streets.

 If someone gives you a helping hand, offer to help them with something else.

Compliment your friends and family. Show them that you care.

 Say thank you to your parents and your elders. You wouldn't be here without them!